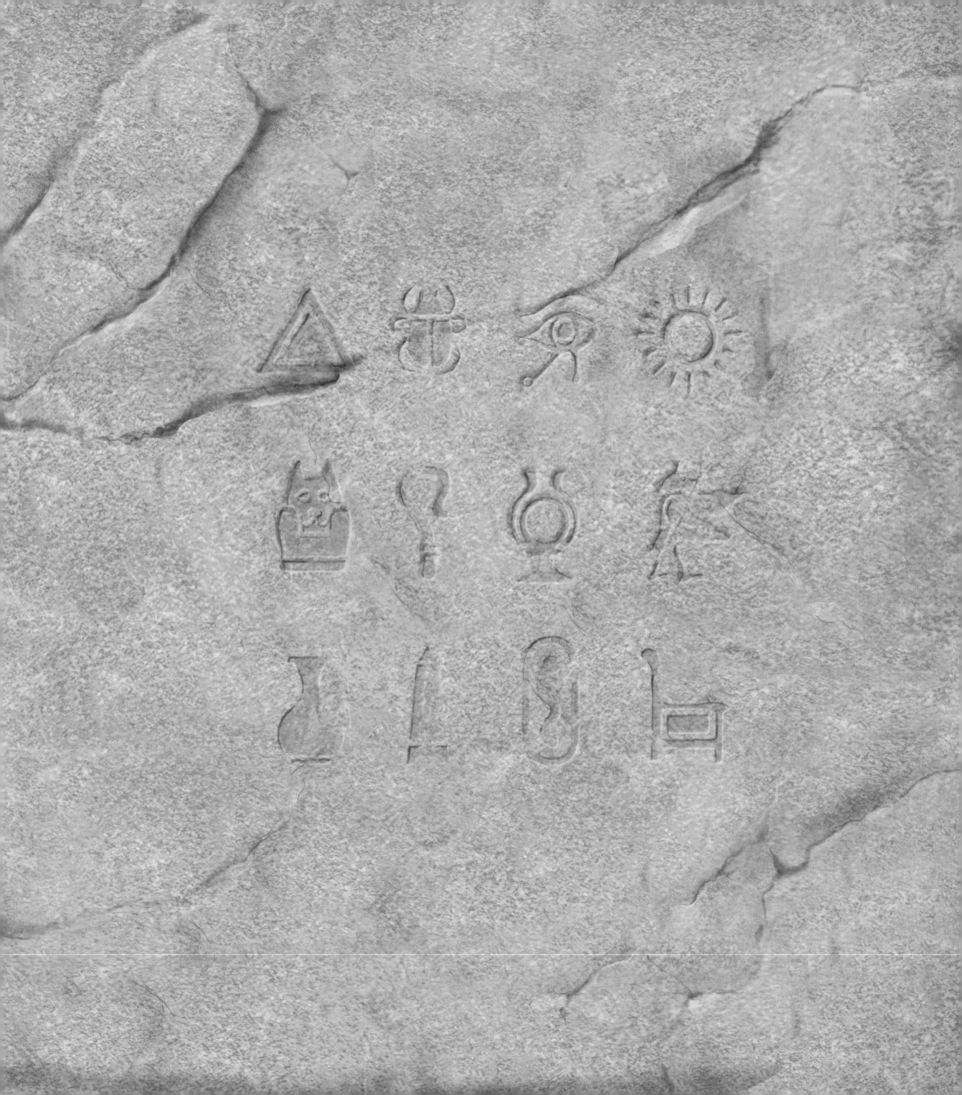

The Jewel Fish of
KARNAK

For Anna and Derek and Jay

Cataloging-in-Publication Data has been applied for and
may be obtained from the Library of Congress.

ISBN for this edition: 978-1-4197-0086-6

Copyright © Doublebase Pty. Ltd., 2011
First published by Penguin Group (Australia), 2011

Printed and bound in China
10 9 8 7 6 5 4 3 2 1

Abrams Books for Young Readers are available at special discounts when
purchased in quantity for premiums and promotions as well as fundraising
or educational use. Special editions can also be created to specification. For
details, contact specialmarkets@abramsbooks.com or the address below.

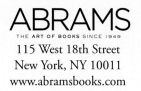

115 West 18th Street
New York, NY 10011
www.abramsbooks.com

The Jewel Fish of KARNAK

Graeme Base

Abrams Books for Young Readers

New York

 ong ago in ancient Egypt, two scruffy thieves called Jackal and Ibis were caught stealing a golden trinket in the marketplace of Asyut. They were brought before the Cat Pharaoh.

"Forgive us, O Pharaoh," they begged. "We are but poor and stupid thieves."

The Cat Pharaoh thought for a moment.

"Well then, thieves, I have a task for you," she said. "In distant Karnak lies the Palace of the Crocodile Prince. Go there and bring back the golden Jewel Fish that the Crocodile took from me. If you do this, I will pardon you."

Jackal and Ibis leapt to their feet. "We will do it!"

he two thieves bowed low to the Cat Pharaoh,
jumped into their little felucca, and set sail.

"Be warned," the Cat Pharaoh told them as they departed.
"Do not take anything else while you are in Karnak. And know
that the Jewel Fish is magical. Be sure it does not get wet."

For many days Jackal and Ibis journeyed up the Nile.

inally, the mighty temple of Karnak came into view. Beside it lay the Palace of the Crocodile Prince. Jackal and Ibis hid their felucca carefully among the reeds and slipped inside.

he Crocodile Prince sat surrounded by his treasure. The sight of all the gold made the two thieves stop and stare. But then they saw the Jewel Fish. It was very beautiful — bright gold and covered in rubies, emeralds, and topaz. They held their breath and slipped it into their sack.

Then without a sound they tiptoed away.

ut at the door they paused, looked at each other, and crept back. They couldn't resist taking some treasures for themselves.

"Just these three," they said as they popped them in their sack. "It can't hurt."

But just then the Crocodile Prince looked up.

"Thieves!" he roared.

he Crocodile chased Jackal and Ibis through the palace.

He chased them through the gardens.

 e chased them all the way back to the river.

"Where did we hide our felucca?" cried Jackal and Ibis. But there was no time to find it. They leapt into a tiny coracle and pushed off into the flowing current.

Soon they had left Karnak far behind.

"We did it!" they laughed. "With the Jewel Fish we shall win the pharaoh's pardon. And with our other little treasures we shall live happily ever after."

But the weight of the extra treasures, along with the Jewel Fish and the two thieves, was too much for the tiny coracle. It began to sink.

Desperate to keep the Jewel Fish dry, as they had been warned, Jackal and Ibis hurled their other treasures overboard. But too late . . .

Water flowed in. The sack was soaked. And before Jackal and Ibis knew what was happening, the Jewel Fish came suddenly to life. It wriggled out of the sack and leapt overboard.

"No!" they cried. And they dived in after it.

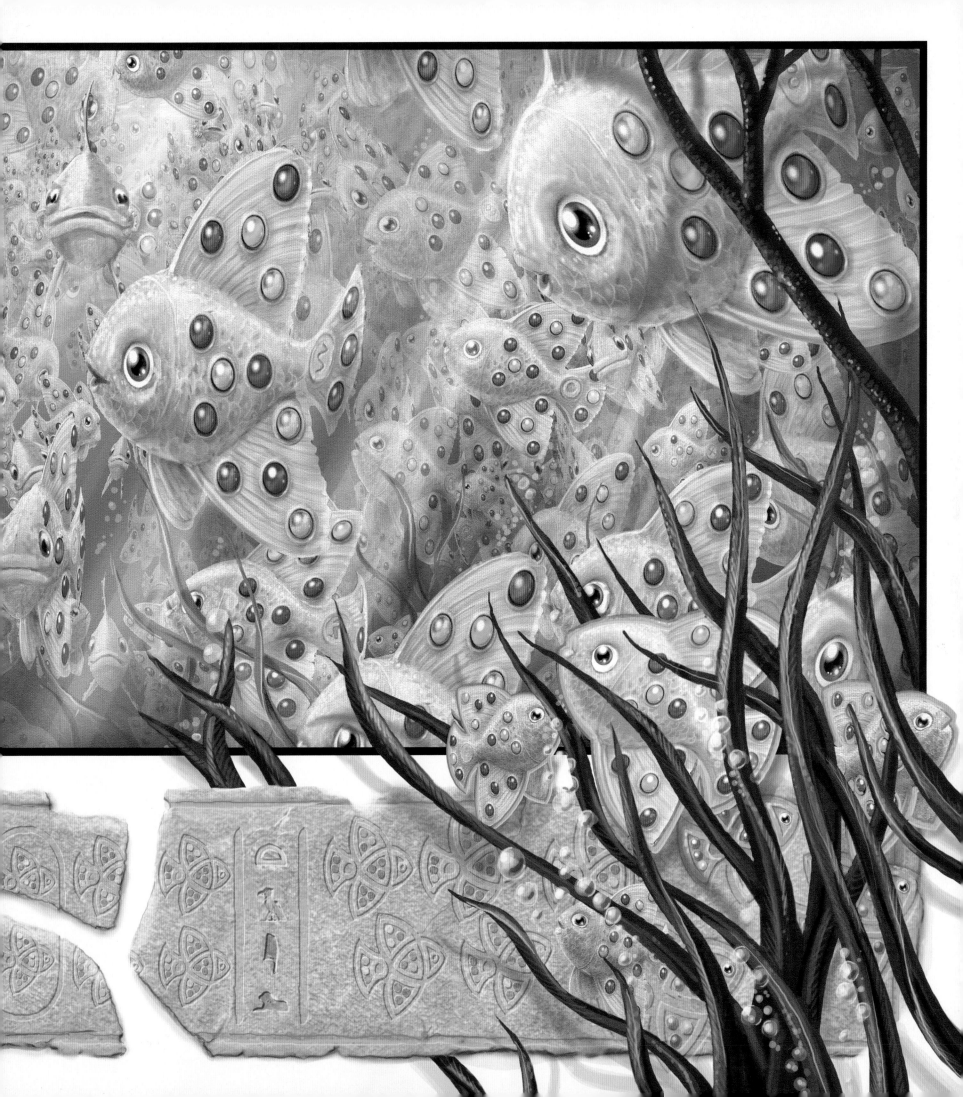

 ackal and Ibis dragged themselves ashore.

"If only we had listened to the pharaoh and not taken anything else," they moaned. "Our treasures are gone. And if we return home without the Jewel Fish, we will surely be punished. Now we have nothing."

They sat on the banks of the River Nile and wept at their stupidity.

fter a while, they dried their tears. "We must go back and confess what we have done."

They made their way back to Asyut and knelt before the pharaoh once again.

"We found the Jewel Fish," they said. "But it got wet and swam away."

They explained what they had done. The Cat Pharaoh was not pleased, but she was impressed that the two thieves had returned to admit their mistake.

"Then you shall have to find it," she told them.

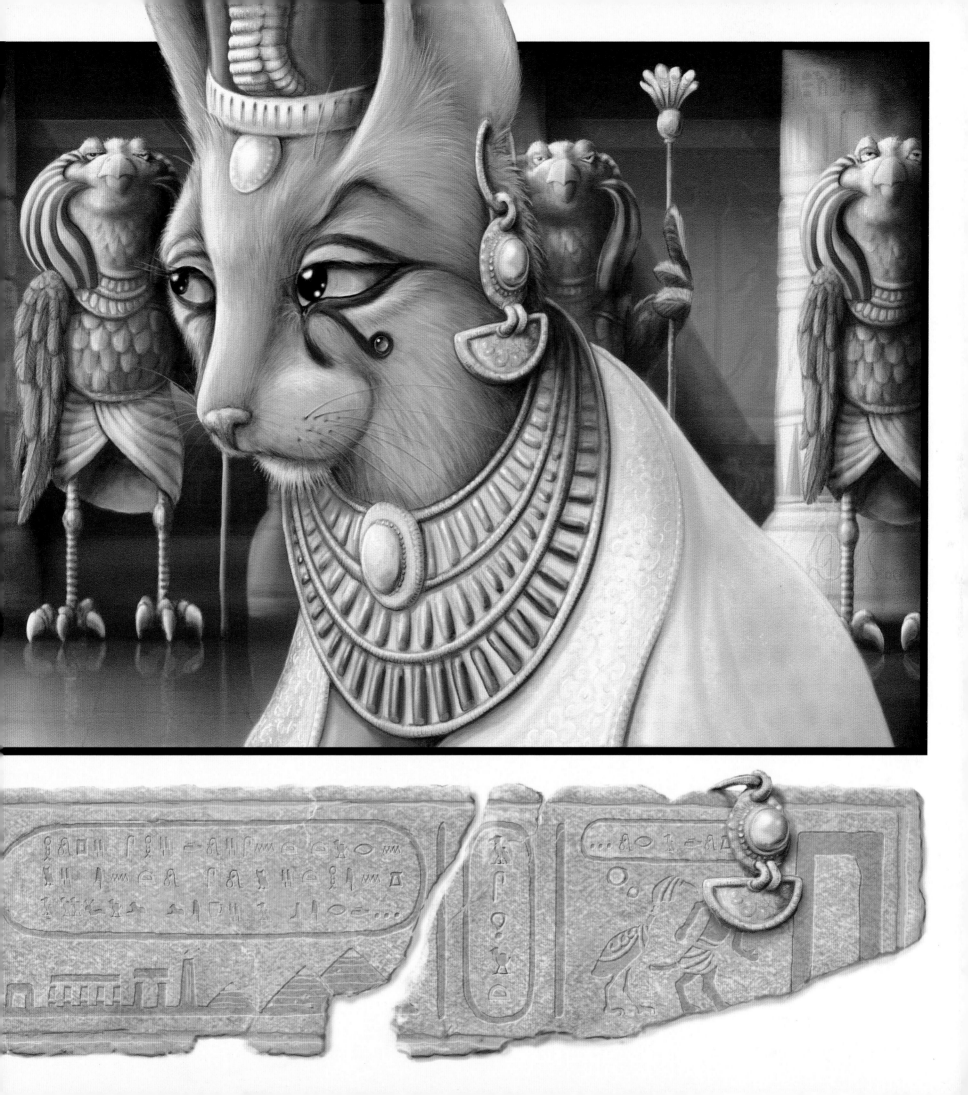

 ackal and Ibis sat on the riverbank and began fishing.

"Perhaps we will find the Jewel Fish," they said to each other. "And when it dries, it will turn back into gold and jewels! Then we can go home and all will be well."

The sun went down over ancient Egypt, and they kept on fishing, hoping to catch the one fish they needed from among all the glittering treasures of the Nile.

And they will probably be fishing there forever.

Unless, of course, you can help them . . . ?

Jackal and Ibis were not very clever, were they?
And finding the Jewel Fish among all the fish
of the Nile would be a very clever trick indeed.

But I am a merciful Cat. If you bring the Jewel Fish to my
palace at www.graemebase.com, I shall release Jackal and
Ibis from their endless task — and reward you as well.

But be warned, I shall demand proof that you have
brought me the right fish!

When you know exactly what the Jewel Fish looks like,
turn the wheels of the ancient mechanism at the back
of the book until you see the correct pattern of jewels.
Thus will the proof I require be revealed.

Good luck on your quest.